Tiny Tim's Christmas Carol

by Ken and Jack Ludwig

based on
A Christmas Carol
by Charles Dickens

A SAMUEL FRENCH ACTING EDITION

FOUNDED 1830

SAMUELFRENCH.COM
SAMUELFRENCH-LONDON.CO.UK

FOR PRODUCTION ENQUIRIES

UNITED STATES AND CANADA
Info@SamuelFrench.com
1-866-598-8449

UNITED KINGDOM AND EUROPE
Plays@SamuelFrench-London.co.uk
020-7255-4302

Each title is subject to availability from Samuel French, depending upon country of performance. Please be aware that *TINY TIM'S CHRISTMAS CAROL* may not be licensed by Samuel French in your territory. Professional and amateur producers should contact the nearest Samuel French office or licensing partner to verify availability.

MUSIC USE NOTE

Licensees are solely responsible for obtaining formal written permission from copyright owners to use copyrighted music in the performance of this play and are strongly cautioned to do so. If no such permission is obtained by the licensee, then the licensee must use only original music that the licensee owns and controls. Licensees are solely responsible and liable for all music clearances and shall indemnify the copyright owners of the play(s) and their licensing agent, Samuel French, against any costs, expenses, losses and liabilities arising from the use of music by licensees. Please contact the appropriate music licensing authority in your territory for the rights to any incidental music.

IMPORTANT BILLING AND CREDIT REQUIREMENTS

If you have obtained performance rights to this title, please refer to your licensing agreement for important billing and credit requirements.

TINY TIM'S CHRISTMAS CAROL was first produced by the Adventure Theatre Musical Theater Center (Michael J. Bobbitt, Producing Artistic Director; Janet Butler Berry, Managing Director) in Glen Echo, Maryland on November 14, 2014. The performance was directed by Jerry Whiddon, with sets by Dan Conway, props and puppetry by Dre Moore, costumes by Collin Ranney, lighting by Martha Mountain, and sound by Neil McFadden. The Production Stage Manager was Donna Stout. The cast was as follows:

TINY TIM	Chris Dinolfo
SCROOGE	Conrad Feininger
CHARLOTTE	Brittany Martz
PUPPET SELLER	Megan Dominy
PIE SELLER	Phil Reid
BOOK SELLER	Danny Pushkin

AUTHORS' NOTE

We wrote this play to try to bring what we believe to be one of the greatest stories in English literature to a young audience, and we tried to envision it through a child's eyes. Scrooge is one of those iconic, mythic figures who will never grow old, and his transformation is perhaps the greatest journey from one who is misguided to one who is good in all of literature. Scrooge's journey is internal – it is a journey of self-knowledge – and through that self-knowledge, he achieves hope for the future, not just for himself but for all mankind. We hope that, by seeing this journey through the eyes of Tiny Tim, there has been a small but newly washed pebble added to the remarkable mountain that is *A Christmas Carol.*

– Ken & Jack Ludwig

For Olivia Ludwig: Best sister, best daughter, best friend.
And for Jerry Whiddon, whose vision brought this play to life.

Scene One

(A street in London in 1843. We're in the commercial district of the city and it's bustling with activity. One of the doors on the street bears a sign that says "SCROOGE and MARLEY.")

*(Among the **LONDONERS**, we see **TINY TIM**, a thoughtful, fresh-faced, optimistic young man of fifteen years. His clothes are respectable, but they're too small for him, and they're slightly tattered from too much wear. We also see his friend **CHARLOTTE**, a year younger, not as poor, but just as resilient. She's pretty, tom-boyish and full of mischief. Finally we see three **STREET SELLERS**, each with his or her own cart. The first is a woman, the **PUPPET SELLER**, and there's something mysterious about her, as though her ancestors may have migrated from the Caribbean and known a little voodoo. Or perhaps she's a gypsy and her magic is Romany in nature. The second of the three is the **PIE SELLER**. He's ruddy and good-natured with a red nose and a large belly. He sells hot pies and other hot victuals because he loves to eat them himself. The third of the three is the **BOOK SELLER**. He has a studious air and wears a battered top hat and a tail coat.)*

(As the audience settles down, these five characters set the scene, greeting the audience with period chatter – and before we realize it, the play has started:)

THE LONDONERS. How have you been keepin', then?
Lookin' forward to Christmas, are ya?
You have a good Christmas, all right? Ya promise?
Brrr.
Cold.
Cold.

Cold in London.

With early dark.

And people hurryin' home to their suppers.

(to each other)

Lemme warm me hands, d'ya mind, m'dear?

O' course not. Be my guest.

The heat is free, cause it comes from his pies!

Ha ha!

It's Christmas!

Christmas.

The lights.

The singin'.

The singin's me favorite part.

Mine too.

And me.

(pitch pipe)

Hmmmm.

(in harmony)

DECK THE HALLS WITH BOUGHS OF HOLLY
FA LA LA LA LA, LA-LA-LA-LA!
TIS THE SEASON TO BE JOLLY
FA LA LA LA LA, LA-LA-LA-LA!
DON WE NOW OUR GAY APPAREL
FA LA LA, LA LA LA, LA, LA, LAAA,
TROLL THE ANCIENT YULE-TIDE CAROL,
FA LA LA LA LAAAA, LA-LA-LA-LAAAA!

*(***TINY TIM*** springs forward.)*

TIM. *(with a slight Cockney accent)* Welcome to London!
My name is Tiny Tim and I've lived here on these
beautiful, crowded, impossibly noisy and windy* streets
since I was born o' me mother's womb just fifteen years
ago and I'm happy to see you. Now I live thataway, on
St. Eustis's Court, about ten streets due North of here,
and while it may not be the fanciest section of this fine

---

*i.e. circuitous, with a long i

old city, we have got what you might call spirit,
and faith,

and confidence that something good's gonna happen
before you know it – and that's an awfully good way to
live your life and I recommend it very highly.

THE STREET SELLERS. Here, here! / Here, here!

CHARLOTTE. Now at the moment the year is 1834 –

TIM. That's my friend Charlotte. You're gonna like her.

CHARLOTTE. – and 1834 is simply a wonderful year to be
living in. It's the time of the horse and buggy,

*(One of the sellers uses coconuts to create the clip-clop
sound of a horse and another one imitates the neigh of a
horse – both of them in view of the audience.)*

the beginning of the steam locomotive –

(Another seller blows a steam whistle.)

– and all over London, right on the streets, there are
men and women selling everything you could ever
think of, from fish to frogs, from toys to togs, from
buttons to books – you name it, they've got it.

PIE SELLER. Hot pies and mulled cider! Get 'em while
they're hot and delicious –

(to the audience)

See I'm the Pie Seller. I bakes the pies, I sells the pies,
and when there's any left, I *eats* the pies, to which I
have no objection whatsoever.

BOOK SELLER. Books for sale! It's the chance of a lifetime!

(to the audience)

I've got histories, mysteries, romance and thrills,
I got comedies, tragedies, weepers and chills.
Read a book a day and become *very smart*.

PUPPET SELLER. Puppets right here for an excellent price!
Who wants a puppet!

(to the audience)

See, I've been makin' puppets since I was six years old,
and some of 'em are me best friends.

CHARLOTTE. Excuse me, madam. Can your puppets sing?

PUPPET SELLER. Can they *sing*? Are you bein' funny? They've been singin' since they was blocks o' wood.

(The three **STREET SELLERS** *operate a chorus line of* **PUPPETS** *who dance and sing:)*

PUPPETS.

WE WISH YOU A MERRY CHRISTMAS,

WE WISH YOU A MERRY CHRISTMAS,

WE WISH YOU A MERRY CHRISTMAS,

AND A HAPPY NEW YEEEEEEEEEAR!

TIM. So there you have it and we're off to a pretty good start.

You've met our friends,

you know we're in London,

you know it's Christmas,

and now I'd like to tell you about another Christmas, a mysterious, exciting, remarkable Christmas just a few short years ago.

(Music plays – "His Yoke is Easy" from Handel's Messiah – and the lights begin to change.)

I was ten years old at the time, and I was still using this crutch to get around. You see I had this disease called rickets, which is something that can get better, or it can get worse, depending on the medicine you take, and because I like to look on the bright side o' things, I grew up having plenty of hope, and that's how it should be. However it kept me mum and dad a bit worried, and they were worried already about feeding the family.

BOOK SELLER. The times were hard.

PIE SELLER. The world was darker.

PUPPET SELLER. We called it The Year of the Scrooge.

(We hear a clap of thunder. And now the lighting and music transition is complete. We are now in the flashback when **TIM** *was ten years old.)*

(**TIM** *sees* **CHARLOTTE** *coming up the street, and he runs up to her.*)

TIM. Charlotte! Have you seen your Uncle Scrooge around?

CHARLOTTE. Not today, thank goodness. Why do you want him?

TIM. I don't want him, I'm trying to avoid him. I want to go see my father and bring him home for Christmas Eve. But you know Scrooge, he'll make some excuse about keeping Father till midnight or something.

CHARLOTTE. Scrooge really is the squeezingest,

TIM. wrenchingest,

CHARLOTTE. graspingest,

TIM. scrapingest,

CHARLOTTE. clutchingest,

TIM. covetous old sinner that ever lived.

(**TIM** *and* **CHARLOTTE** *shudder – as* **SCROOGE** *appears, little by little, looming up behind them.*)

Do you know what somebody said the other day? They said that Scrooge carried his own low temperature inside him.

CHARLOTTE. Ha! It sort of freezes his features,

TIM. and cramps his nose,

CHARLOTTE. and shrivels his cheek,

TIM. and makes his eyes bloodshot,

CHARLOTTE. and his thin lips blue.

(**SCROOGE** *is right behind them now.*)

TIM. Do you know, I'd say he's the ugliest old man that I've ever –

BOTH. *AGH!!*

SCROOGE. And to whom may I ask were you referring?

TIM. My-my-my-my godfather.

CHARLOTTE. His godfather!

TIM. His name is Barnaby.   **CHARLOTTE.** Aloysius.
                                    [pronounced "Allo-wishus"]

TIM. Barnaby Aloysius Cratchit. You'd really like him.

CHARLOTTE. Except he's mean –

TIM. – and *stingy* –

CHARLOTTE. – and not like you at all!

TIM. We've got to go now.

CHARLOTTE. Bye!

TIM. G'bye!

SCROOGE. Bah, humbug!

(They rush off down the street – and **TINY TIM** *addresses the audience:)*

TIM. And that was the day that changed everything. It was Christmas Eve and I was on my way to surprise my father at work and walk home with him so we could get Christmas started –

(Two **CHARITY COLLECTORS** *have appeared, walking up the street. Their names are* **STEVENS** *and* **HOLLYFOOT**. *They have books and papers in their hands.)*

STEVENS. Ah ha!

HOLLYFOOT. That's him.

STEVENS. I'm sure it is!

HOLLYFOOT. I'm positive!

TIM. – and I saw two men who were collecting for the poor and homeless go up to Scrooge and ask him for money.

STEVENS. Excuse us sir. I'm Stevens.

HOLLYFOOT. I'm Hollyfoot.

STEVENS. And I believe we have seen you coming out of Scrooge and Marley's Counting House on several occasions.

SCROOGE. So what? What about it?

HOLLYFOOT. Have we the pleasure of addressing Mr. Scrooge or Mr. Marley?

SCROOGE. Mr. Marley, my former partner, has been dead as a doornail these seven years. In fact he died seven years ago this very night. Now what do you want?

STEVENS. We are here to collect for charity, sir.

HOLLYFOOT. To help the starving,

STEVENS. and the destitute.

HOLLYFOOT. You see, a few of us are trying to raise money for the poor, to buy them food and blankets during the Christmas season. Now what do you say?

SCROOGE. Are there no prisons?

STEVENS. ...Prisons, sir?

SCROOGE. Are there no workhouses?

HOLLYFOOT. I'm sure that you don't mean that, sir.

STEVENS. *(pen poised)* So how much money would you like to contribute?

SCROOGE. None.

HOLLYFOOT. Ah, I see. You wish to remain anonymous, then.

SCROOGE. I wish to be left alone!! I do not make merry myself at Christmas, and I can't afford to make the idle merry!

STEVENS. But many would rather die than go to prison, sir.

SCROOGE. If they would rather die, they had better do it and *decrease the surplus population!*

(He looks at his watch.)

Oh, now look what you've done. I'm going to be late getting back to work and Cratchit may have left already to start his holiday!

TIM. Oh, no!

(to the audience)

I realized in a flash that I had to get my father out of there!

(TIM runs off.)

Scene Two

(Inside Scrooge and Marley's Counting House. **BOB**
CRATCHIT, *Tiny Tim's kindly father, is on a stool at
a little desk with a quill pen in his hand, doing the
account books. He's very cold, with only the candle on
his desk to keep him warm.)*

TIM. Father! Father! Scrooge is coming, you've gotta go
quick!

BOB. Tim, my wonderful boy, what are you doing here?

TIM. Please hurry, pack up! If he finds you still here on
Christmas Eve he'll make you stay later and later
and Mother's got the roast in the oven and Martha's
arrived and Emily's already setting the table!

BOB. But Tim, I can't just leave my desk without permission.
It isn't right.

TIM. But Father –

BOB. I'm sorry, Tim, but I work for Mr. Scrooge and I owe
him a certain amount of respect. And so do you.

SCROOGE. *(off) Bah, humbug.*

TIM. *Here he comes!*

(TIM *springs into a hiding place behind a trunk or a
stove. The moment he's hidden,* **SCROOGE** *enters.)*

SCROOGE. Cratchit!

BOB. Yes sir?

SCROOGE. Are you finished with the accounts?

BOB. Almost, sir.

SCROOGE. "Almost?"

BOB. Yes, sir. You see my fingers get stiff with the cold and I
can't work as fast as I'd like to. But if I could put a little
coal on the fire –

SCROOGE. "Coal" did you say?

BOB. Yes sir. Coal.

SCROOGE. Coal costs money. When I was a lad I had no coal
and I did perfectly well without it. Do you understand?

BOB. *(shivering)* Yes, sir.

(TIM *stands up and shakes his fist at* SCROOGE, *but* SCROOGE *can't see him.* BOB *motions to* TIM *to stay down – and* TIM *disappears just as* SCROOGE *turns around.*)

SCROOGE. Use the candle to warm yourself, Cratchit. But don't use much of it. Candles cost money too, you know.

(*Jingle! It is the sound of the door opening, and* FRED *and his daughter* CHARLOTTE *walk in.* FRED *is middle-aged and wonderfully cheerful.*)

FRED. Merry Christmas, Uncle!

SCROOGE. Bah, humbug.

FRED. You remember my daughter Charlotte, of course.

CHARLOTTE. Merry Christmas Great Uncle Scrooge.

SCROOGE. Would you all stop saying Merry Christmas! There is nothing merry about it!

FRED. Now Uncle Scrooge, you don't mean that.

SCROOGE. Of course I do. What right have you to be merry? You're poor enough.

FRED. What right have you to be dismal? You're rich enough.

TIM. (*from his hiding place*) Ha ha! Good one!

(SCROOGE *whips around and looks in* TIM's *direction.* CHARLOTTE *saves the day by changing her voice to sound like* TIM *and cries:*)

CHARLOTTE. "Ha ha! Good one!"

FRED. Don't be cross, Uncle.

SCROOGE. What else can I be when I live in such a world of fools. "Merry Christmas." What's Christmas time to you but a time for paying bills without money, hanh? If I had my way, every idiot who goes about with "Merry Christmas" on his lips should be boiled in his own pudding and buried with a stake of holly through his heart.

FRED. I'm sorry that you feel that way, Uncle.

(Music plays: The Third (Adagio) Movement of Haydn String Quartet Opus 64, No. 4 in G Major)

I'm here as usual to invite you to our family party, and we hope you'll join us tomorrow and raise a cup to good fellowship. I have always thought of Christmas as a forgiving, charitable time when men and women, by one consent, open their hearts and do kindness to others. And although it has never put a scrap of gold or silver in my pocket, I believe that Christmas has done me good, and does all of us good, and I say God bless it.

*(**CHARLOTTE** bursts into applause. Then **BOB** does too. Then **TIM** springs up from his hiding place and applauds vigorously as well. **SCROOGE** again whips around, and again just misses **TIM**, who drops back into hiding.)*

SCROOGE. *(to **FRED**) You*, sir, may leave my office, and I refuse to go to your ridiculous party.

*(to **BOB**)*

And *you*, sir, may clear out for the day because I want you back here tomorrow morning at nine o'clock.

BOB. But it's Christmas Day!

SCROOGE. "But it's Christmas Day." And I suppose you want to be *paid* for it.

BOB. But it is traditional…

SCROOGE. Tradition be damned! Christmas is a poor excuse for picking a man's pocket every twenty-fifth of December and I will not have it!

*(**TIM** springs up from behind his hiding place and declares to **SCROOGE**:)*

TIM. That's unfair!

SCROOGE. Who's that?

BOB CRATCHIT. Uh, that is my son, sir. And I apologize for his poor behavior.

CHARLOTTE. You *shouldn't* apologize. It is unfair and you shouldn't agree to work on Christmas! And he shouldn't speak to my father that way!

BOB/FRED. Tim! / Charlotte!

SCROOGE. *How dare you children! Get out! Get out I say!*

(**SCROOGE** *chases them around his office.*)

TIM. *Help!*

CHARLOTTE. *Stop it!*

BOB. *Tim!*

FRED. *Charlotte!*

SCROOGE. *Out! Out!*

(*A chase ensues, and the* **CHILDREN** *exit at a run.*)

Scene Three

(The street, as **TIM** *and* **CHARLOTTE** *run to the corner, bursting with anger.)*

TIM. I think we lost him!

(They pant from the run.)

CHARLOTTE. He's awful!

TIM. He's cruel!

CHARLOTTE. He's mean!

TIM. I don't like him!

CHARLOTTE. If you ask me, he needs a lesson. Except *he's* an adult and *we're* children and I haven't the faintest idea what to do!

(pant, pant)

TIM. He must have had an awful childhood.

CHARLOTTE. He did.

(Beat. **TIM** *looks at* **CHARLOTTE**.*)*

TIM. What do you mean "he did?"

CHARLOTTE. I mean he did. He had an awful childhood. His father sent him to boarding school to be rid of him. And he was almost married but his fiancé left him.

TIM. How do you know all this?

CHARLOTTE. He's my father's uncle. Family stories. We talk about him all the time.

(Beat.)

TIM. …Charlotte?

CHARLOTTE. Yes, Tim.

TIM. I think I'm getting an idea… But we'd need some help.

CHARLOTTE. What kind of help?

TIM. Well… I think we'd need someone who could make some costumes and was good at creating things.

PUPPET SELLER. *(entering with the other* **SELLERS***)* Puppets! Puppets! Hand-made puppets in beautiful costumes!

TIM. Then I think we'd need someone who could write a story – who was really clever because he'd read so much.

BOOK SELLER. Books! Books! Don't be shy! We've got Homer and Chaucer and Shakespeare and Dickens!

TIM. And finally we'd need a really marvelous actor who could spin a tale and could give you confidence and do lots and lots of different voices.

PIE SELLER. Pies for sale! The best bloomin' pies ever baked in the history of this fine old world, fresh as a meadow and tasty as a clam, and as my darlin' mother used to say

(with his mother's voice:)

"Why Simon, there is nobody in London who makes pies like you!"

*(***TIM*** and ***CHARLOTTE*** turn and look at each other…)*

TIM/CHARLOTTE. Ha ha! / Let's try it!

TIM. Friends, please join us and gather 'round. We have a little proposition to make.

(They get into a huddle and start whispering)

PIE SELLER. What?!

BOOK SELLER. Oh, good!

PUPPET SELLER. Do what?

PIE SELLER. Do *what?!*

TIM. We scare Scrooge.

PIE SELLER. Scare Scrooge?

PIE SELLER. He tried to cheat me once!

BOOK SELLER. And me.

PUPPET SELLER. And me.

PIE SELLER. But how do we do it?!

(Circle. Buzz, buzz, buzz, buzz!)

PUPPET SELLER. Costumes?

PIE SELLER. And lights?

CHARLOTTE. And sounds.

TIM. And stories!

BOOK SELLER. Ha ha!

PUPPET SELLER. That's good.

PIE SELLER. That's excellent!

TIM. So what do you say?

ALL THREE SELLERS. *We're in!*

TIM. *(to the audience:)* And so Charlotte and I and our friends from the streets came up with a plan to teach Scrooge a lesson he would never, ever forget.

(A blast of rousing, exciting music plays. The FRIENDS walk off buzzing happily: "Excellent!" "Superb!" "I adore it!" Meanwhile, with a change of sound and light, the story of Scrooge's transformation begins.)

Scene Four

(In front of Scrooge's House. We're at the door.)

SCROOGE. Bah, humbug!

(imitating the voices of the goody-goodies)

"It's Christmas time so give us some money." "Peace on Earth, we want more money." "Deck the halls with boughs of" *what's the matter with these people!* All this fuss because the calendar says it's the twenty-fourth day of December? Oh, please. As my old partner Jacob Marley used to say "Spare me the sentiment. If you want to shed a tear, then go out in the lobby." Ha!… Wait. I have an idea. Let's take a vote. Raise your hand if you agree with me that *children should never get any presents at Christmas time.* Do we all agree? No presents?

(He raises his own hand – but no one else does.)

You're doing this on purpose, aren't you? O *tempora o mores. Oh the times, the customs!* I simply hate to think what this younger generation is coming to. Gimme, gimme. Food, food. Water, water. Talk about selfish. All I need is my home. My hearth. And here it is in front of me. Do you see it? This is my stoop, this is my railing, this is my door and this is my doorknocker. *AGHHHHHHH!*

(The cause of the scream is that the doorknocker is now the head of **SCROOGE***'s old partner,* **JACOB MARLEY***. Note: this is the real head of the* **PIE SELLER***, sticking out through a cutout in the door.)*

Did you see that?!

(It changes back, but **SCROOGE** *doesn't see it.)*

Since when does a doorknocker look like Jacob Marley?! The man's been dead for seven years! Look, look, it's unbelievable! It looks exactly like my old partner, Jacob Ma –

(The knocker is back to normal by this time.)

...What happened? It's a doorknocker. I'd like to knock some heads with this knocker here. A trick of the light! That's all it was. Of course. The light. Puh. Look for yourselves. Whew. It's nothing but a good old-fashioned, everyday door knyyyaAAA*AGHHHHHHH!*

(It has turned to **MARLEY** *again. The change happens while* **SCROOGE** *is looking away.)*

It's Marley! It's Marley! But Marley is dead! He's been dead as a doornail these seven years, so how could he possibly be right over...

(But now the doorknocker is back to normal. **SCROOGE** *gasps. Then, to the audience:)*

Are you doing this to me?

(to someone in the front row:)

Is it you?... Well stop it... I'll use my key.

(He takes out a key, inserts it in the lock and we hear the loud sound of the key turning. Then the bolts going back and the ominous sound of the door squeaking on its hinges, then closing with a bang.)

(And now we're inside Scrooge's house along with **SCROOGE**. *The primary thing we see is Scrooge's bed. It's a lumpy mattress on an old fashioned bedstead, with an old tattered sheet and a pathetic old pillow.)*

Ahhh. Home. What more do I need. I love routine. Every night it is the same procedure:

(He does the actions he describes:)

I light my candle. I have my bowl of thin gruel. (You should try it some time, it is quite delicious.) I have my luscious glass of tap water.

(He makes noises as he drinks.)

I put on my trusty nightgown and cap. I lie down gently on my favorite sheet... and I dream of money.

(He closes his eyes and starts to snore. After a beat, we hear thunder, along with the clanking of chains and the moaning of a **GHOST.***)*

(And we see **TIM** *and* **CHARLOTTE** *at the side of the stage creating the sounds with heavy chains and a wind machine.)*

MARLEY'S GHOST. *Scrooooooooooooge! Scrooooooooooooge!*

*(***SCROOGE** *opens his eyes, and out of the darkness comes* **THE GHOST OF JACOB MARLEY**. *He is played by the* **PIE SELLER**.*)*

Scrooooooooooooge!

SCROOGE. *Agh! Who are you?!*

MARLEY'S GHOST. Ask me who I was!

SCROOGE. Who were you then?

MARLEY'S GHOST. In life I was your partner, Jacob Marley.

SCROOGE. Are you a ghost?

MARLEY'S GHOST. Of course I'm a ghost. Why do you ask?

SCROOGE. Because disorders of the stomach can affect the brain. You could be a bit of undigested beef I had for lunch. Or a blot of mustard, or a crumb of cheese. There is more of gravy than of grave about you, whocvcr you arc.

MARLEY'S GHOST. *I AM MARLEY'S GHOST!!!*

(It is a huge loud cry, accompanied by thunder and lightning.)

(And we see **TIM** *and* **CHARLOTTE** *off to the side using a bass drum, lightning sheet, etc. for the sound and light effects.* **SCROOGE** *cowers in fear.)*

SCROOGE. Aghhhhh! Why do you wear chains, Jacob?

MARLEY'S GHOST. I wear the chains I forged in life. They represent my indifference to those who suffered around me.

SCROOGE. But you were always a good man of business, Jacob.

MARLEY'S GHOST. Mankind should have been my business, Ebeznezer, but I ignored it. Now mark me. I am here tonight to tell you that you yet have a chance of escaping my fate. And to that end, this night you will be haunted by Three Spirits.

SCROOGE. I-I-I'd rather not meet them, if you don't mind. I-I-I'm really quite busy this evening and I'm sure they'd understand if I –

MARLEY'S GHOST. *THREE SPIRITS!!!*

(Again we hear a huge sound of thunder and lightning created by **TIM** *and* **CHARLOTTE**. *Only this time,* **TIM** *drops the bass drum on* **CHARLOTTE***'s toe and she screams.)*

CHARLOTTE. Ouch! Would you watch where you're…!

(They realize their gaff and try to look invisible – and the **GHOST** *tries to cover for them as well. Fortunately,* **SCROOGE** *doesn't catch on to them.)*

Expect the first ghost tonight when the bell tolls one. The second at two, and the third at three. These three spirits and the messages they bring you are your only hope.

SCROOGE. Hope? Hope of what? Why do I need hope?

MARLEY'S GHOST. Why do any of us need hope in life, Ebenezer Scrooooooge.

(Thunder, but now rolling and distant, and **MARLEY** *starts to fade away.)*

SCROOGE. Jacob, please. Stay with me a little longer.

MARLEY'S GHOST. Remember me. Remember me. Remember me.

(And now the room is back the way it was. **SCROOGE** *takes a deep breath.)*

SCROOGE. Well. Everything seems quite normal again. Here's my pillow. Here's my sheet. Here's my gruel. Hmm. A ghost? Nonsense.

Was that really a ghost or a piece of toast?

Or a celery stalk pretending to talk?

Or a marmalade who began to fade?

Or a bottle of stout who had the gout?

Or a mess of livers who gave me the shivers?! Ha ha!

It sounds like a lot of hogwash to me. "Three Spirits." Stuff and nonsense. It's time for bed. I'll listen to the carolers in the street. It will lull me to sleep.

CAROLERS.

THE HOLLY AND THE IVY,

WHEN THEY ARE BOTH FULL GROWN,

OF ALL THE TREES THAT ARE IN THE WOOD,

THE HOLLY BEARS THE CROWN.

OH, THE RISING OF THE SUN

AND THE RUNNING OF THE DEER,

THE PLAYING OF THE MERRY ORGAN,

SWEET SINGING IN THE CHOIR –

(**SCROOGE** *falls asleep on his bed and begins to snore. Then* **TIM** *hits a gong that sounds like a clock striking one o'clock.*)

SCROOGE. Hm?! What? What's happening?!

Scene Five

(Continuous.)

*(***THE GHOST OF CHRISTMAS PAST*** *appears. It is the* ***PUPPET SELLER*** *– or a puppet manipulated by the* ***PUPPET SELLER.****)*

THE GHOST OF CHRISTMAS PAST. *Ebeneeeeeeezer Scroooooooge. Ebeneeeeeeezer Scroooooooge.*

SCROOGE. *Agh!!! Who are you?!!*

THE GHOST OF CHRISTMAS PAST. I am the Ghost of Christmas Past.

SCROOGE. Long past?

THE GHOST OF CHRISTMAS PAST. No. Your past. Now rise and walk with me. We shall visit your history.

SCROOGE. Walk? Walk where? My bedroom isn't very large. Where can I walk to?

THE GHOST OF CHRISTMAS PAST. Walk out the window, Ebenezer.

SCROOGE. Out the window?! That's ridiculous! It's two stories up. I'd kill myself.

THE GHOST OF CHRISTMAS PAST. Trust me, Ebenezer.

SCROOGE. But you don't understand, it's two stories u –

THE GHOST OF CHRISTMAS PAST. *Just trust me, you old fool, and get moving!*

(The ***GHOST*** *takes* ***SCROOGE****'s hand and leads him forward out his window.)*

*(***TIM*** *and* ***CHARLOTTE*** *have arranged a plank for him to walk upon. And the other* ***SELLERS*** *are helping to create the illusion that he is high up in the air – with a wind machine, or, failing that, hand-held fans to create a breeze in his hair, the sounds of the street down below, etc. All of it is to give him the illusion that he is travelling through the air and across time.)*

Do you feel the wind in your hair?

SCROOGE. Yes! I feel it!

THE GHOST OF CHRISTMAS PAST. Do you hear the street below you?

(The **BOOK SELLER** *is operating the coconut shells again.)*

SCROOGE. I do! I do!

THE GHOST OF CHRISTMAS PAST. And now we're entering the countryside where you grew up, which of course was called...

*(***CHARLOTTE** *whispers in the* **PUPPET SELLER**'s *ear.)*

CHARLOTTE. Devonshire.

GHOST. Devonshire

SCROOGE. That's right, that's right!

GHOST. In the town of...

TIM. *(whispering)* Exbourne.

GHOST. Exbourne.

SCROOGE. Yes of course it was!

THE GHOST OF CHRISTMAS PAST. Do you hear the birds in the trees?

*(***TIM** *blows into one of those little contraptions that makes bird-song as you blow through it.)*

SCROOGE. Devonshire birds! Like when I was a boy. And look, there's the old pie seller of my youth!

(The **PIE SELLER***, who's eating some pie, looks around, not expecting to be seen.)*

PIE SELLER. Huh?

SCROOGE. When I was a boy I would sneak past him every Christmas to get a taste of one of his wonderful pies. Oh, happy day!

PIE SELLER. *(offering the half of a pie that's left)* Blueberry Pie! Half off!

SCROOGE. And there's the house where I grew! At least until...until my father sent me away to school. A lonely school where I was a boarder and had no friends.

(At the side of the stage, **CHARLOTTE** *creates the sound of a school bell ringing.)*

SCROOGE. *(cont.)* How I hated the sound of that wretched bell when I was young.

(He sees a **BOY**, *sitting alone. It is* **YOUNG SCROOGE**.*)*

*(***SCROOGE***'s eyes begin to fill with tears. His voice catches in his throat.)*

Spirit. That boy there. Sitting, all alone and silent. Is it me?

GHOST. *It is.*

*(***YOUNG SCROOGE*** is played by* **TIM**.*)*

SCROOGE. There was a girl singing a Christmas carol at my door last night. She seemed quite poor. I wish I had given her something.

GIRL ON THE STREET.

OH, THE RISING OF THE SUN,
AND THE RUNNING OF THE DEER,
THE PLAYING OF THE MERRY ORGAN,
SWEET SINGING IN THE CHOIR.

GHOST. Come. Let us see another Christmas past, when you had grown into a fine young man.

(Music! We're in the middle of a party given by the **FEZZIWIGS**. *Music and dancing. The music is the Gigue from Handel's Music for the Royal Fireworks.* **FEZZIWIG** *and* **MRS. FEZZIWIG** *are dancing up a storm, and* **YOUNG SCROOGE** *is eyeing* **BELLE**, *who is played by* **CHARLOTTE**. **FEZZIWIG** *is played by the* **PIE SELLER** *and* **MRS. FEZZIWIG** *is played by the* **BOOK SELLER** *in drag.)*

SCROOGE. It's Fezziwig's house! My first employer. What a good man he was. He treated me like his own son.

Dear old Fezzi. How he and his wife loved to dance at Christmas…

(When the dance ends:)

FEZZIWIG. *(with an Irish accent, to* **YOUNG SCROOGE***)* Faith and begorah! Ebenezer. You're a good lad and a hard worker. But don't you be workin' on Christmas Eve.

MRS. FEZZIWIG. And there's a young lady named Belle who I spy in the corner who just might be wanting to dance with you. Halllooo.

(Shyly, **YOUNG SCROOGE** *approaches* **BELLE***. So does* **OLD SCROOGE***.)*

YOUNG SCROOGE/OLD SCROOGE. Hello. / Hello.

BELLE. *(to* **YOUNG SCROOGE***)* How do you do.

YOUNG SCROOGE. My name is –

OLD SCROOGE. – Ebenezer.

BELLE. *(to* **YOUNG SCROOGE***)* It's lovely to meet you.

YOUNG SCROOGE. May I have the pleasure?

BELLE. I'd be delighted.

OLD SCROOGE. *(as* **YOUNG SCROOGE** *walks* **BELLE** *to the dance floor)* Spirit, does she not see me?

GHOST. These are but shadows of the things that have been. They have no consciousness of us.

*(***OLD SCROOGE** *lets out a cry of pain as the young* **COUPLE** *dances with joy. At the end they embrace.)*

BELLE. Ebenezer!

YOUNG SCROOGE. Belle! My darling!

BELLE. Oh tell me that this will never change. That we will always be together like this!

YOUNG SCROOGE. Well of course we will. Why shouldn't we be?

MRS. FEZZIWIG. Presents! It's time for presents!

("Hurray!")

This is for you, and this if for you, and this is for you, and this is for…

(As she fades away, the stage darkens and the wind changes.)

SCROOGE. Brr. What's happened? Why is it so cold suddenly?

GHOST. It is time to look at another Christmas.

CHARLOTTE. *(to the audience)* And so we move forward another five years as Scrooge loses sight of the care of his soul.

*(And now **YOUNG SCROOGE** is sitting at a desk, counting his money, putting coins in piles. Clink, clink, clink, clink...)*

SCROOGE. One, two, seven, carry the four...good. Four times six makes 24, and then we add five...

*(**YOUNG SCROOGE** is older than he was, and after a moment, **BELLE** enters.)*

BELLE. Ebenezer?

YOUNG SCROOGE. What?! Belle, what do you want?!

BELLE. Won't you join us at the Fezziwigs' party?

YOUNG SCROOGE. No time, no time. It's business first, you know the rule.

BELLE. But it's Christmas Eve!

YOUNG SCROOGE. There's work to do.

BELLE. But Ebenezer –

SCROOGE. But nothing!... Darling... Don't you realize that Christmas is the perfect time to make a profit. People spend too much! They get carried away!

BELLE. But isn't there time for charity as well?

SCROOGE. "Charity?" Never heard of it. It doesn't pay bills, you can't save it, and you certainly can't spend it. Don't speak to me of "charity."

(to himself:)

One, two, seven, carry the four...

*(**BELLE** turns away.)*

BELLE. Goodbye Ebenezer.

YOUNG SCROOGE. *(absently)* Good night, my dear… Divide by two and carry the six…

CHARLOTTE. *(to the audience)* And Belle walked out of his life forever.

(She walks away and **YOUNG SCROOGE** *barely notices. But* **OLD SCROOGE** *is in agony.)*

SCROOGE. Please! No more! I cannot look! Take me home and haunt me no longer!

TIM. *(to the audience)* And the Ghost of Christmas Past led Mr. Scrooge back to his bedroom –

SCROOGE. No more, no more…

TIM. – and Scrooge then took to his bed again and receded into a profound sleep.

SCROOGE. *Zzzzzzzz!*

Scene Six

(Continuous. **TIM** *confers with his fellow conspirators. The* **PIE SELLER** *is pulling on his costume as* **THE GHOST OF CHRISTMAS PRESENT**. *He's meant to look like a giant, so he has high platform shoes; also a green robe with fur trimming, a crown of holly, and he carries a mutton leg. They all whisper.)*

PIE SELLER. Why does it have to be *me* again?

CHARLOTTE. Because *he's* playing Cratchit so he can't play the ghost. And besides, we need someone to fit this robe.

PIE SELLER. Oh thanks a lot.

TIM. Is the light ready yet?

PIE SELLER. I'm ready when you are.

CHARLOTTE. What about the music?

BOOK SELLER. Ready to go.

TIM. All right, let's do it.

*(*TIM *hits a gong – Bong! Bong! – to sound like the clock striking two – and suddenly the stage is flooded with a bright white light and we hear a resounding excerpt from "The Messiah": the opening seconds of the orchestral section of "Worthy is the Lamb." The effect awakens* SCROOGE, *and he snorts so loudly that he scares himself.)*

SCROOGE. *ZZZT!...* Agh! What happened?... Oh no. It must be the second *aghhh! Who are you?!!*

GHOST. *(full of good cheer)* Good evening, Master Scrooge, it's lovely to meet you. I am the Ghost of...

(He's forgotten.)

...Sorry, one moment.

(He holds his brow.)

I am the Ghost of...

TIM. *(hissing)* Christmas Present!

GHOST. …*of Christmas Present.* And let me say how much I love a good present. A book, a model train, a pair of suspenders…

TIM. Not that kind of present!

GHOST. Oh, right, right, right! What am I thinking? Ha ha! Heh, heh! Ahem.

I am the Ghost of the Here and Now and I am here to take you on a journey now. So touch my robe.

SCROOGE. You know I learned quite a lot on my first journey, and I-I'd just as soon stay right where I –

GHOST. *(getting into the role) Touch my robe.*

(He does.)

Now close your eyes and jump.

SCROOGE. Jump?

GHOST. One, two, three… *JUMP!*

(Holding hands, the two **MEN** *jump a foot or two forward – and they are now at the home of Bob Cratchit.)*

SCROOGE. Where are we?

GHOST. Is this not the home of your assistant Cratchit?

SCROOGE. Why yes it is! On Christmas Eve! And there is his wife cooking supper!

(The **PUPPET SELLER** *plays* **MRS. CRATCHIT**, *Bob's wife, and* **CHARLOTTE** *plays the daughter* **EMILY**.*)*

EMILY. Mother, Mother, I'm home!

SCROOGE. And there's his daughter!

MRS. CRATCHIT. Emily, darling! How late you are! Did you see your father and brother on the way?

EMILY. I did.

TIM. *(entering)* We're home! We're home on Christmas Eve!

MRS. CRATCHIT. And how did my little Tim behave?

BOB. As good as gold. However he was a little forward with Mr. Scrooge this afternoon.

TIM. He's making father work on Christmas Day.

EMILY. No!

MRS. CRATCHIT. He wouldn't dare!

BOB. I'm afraid it's true.

MRS. CRATCHIT. The man's a fiend. I hate him!

BOB. Martha!

MRS. CRATCHIT. Well I'm sorry, but he has done nothing but make your life more difficult.

BOB. That isn't so! He is my – employer and provides us money enough to live. And life, after all, is the greatest of gifts; and so I say we should lift a glass to Mr. Scrooge and call him the Founder of the Feast... Come on, come on.

TIM/EMILY. ...The Founder of the Feast!

MRS. CRATCHIT. I wish I had him here to feast upon, the odious, stingy, unfeeling devil.

BOB. Martha, please!

MRS. CRATCHIT. Oh I'll drink his health for your sake, husband.

BOB. Thank you.

EMILY. Cheers.

MRS. CRATCHIT. Cheers.

BOB. To Mr. Scrooge.

TIM. God bless us, every one. And a special thanks to Mr. Scrooge for making me run today and get all that exercise.

(He taps his leg.)

MRS. CRATCHIT. Now that's our boy.

SCROOGE. Spirit, tell me. Will Tim get better?

(The **PIE SELLER** *is touched and says what he really thinks:)*

GHOST. I see a vacant seat in the chimney corner, and if these shadows remain unaltered by the Future, the child will die.

SCROOGE. Oh no! Oh Spirit say he will be spared!

GHOST. But wouldn't you rather "decrease the surplus population?"

SCROOGE. Forgive me! Please! I shouldn't have said it!

TIM. *(to the audience)* And on we went to Scrooge's nephew's house – or so he believed – and there the annual Christmas party was under way – the one that Scrooge had refused to attend. And one of Fred's nieces was playing quietly upon the piano:

(We hear the music: a simple, touching keyboard air of great beauty: the Arietta from Grieg's Lyric Pieces, Opus 12, No. 1.)

And when this strain of music sounded, all the things that the Ghosts had shown to Scrooge came upon his mind, and he softened more and more and thought that if he could have listened to this music often, years ago, he might have cultivated the kindnesses of life that he so recently had lacked.

(The mood changes.)

When the Ghost of Christmas Present had long since departed, and should have been replaced by Christmas Future, Charlotte and I realized suddenly that we had a problem…

CHARLOTTE. Okay, where is he?

TIM. Where's who?

CHARLOTTE. The next ghost.

TIM. What ghost?

CHARLOTTE. Your ghost.

TIM. I don't have a ghost.

CHARLOTTE. Of course you have a ghost!

TIM. You mean Christmas Future?

CHARLOTTE. Of course. Where is he?

TIM. I thought you were doing him.

CHARLOTTE. You said you were doing him!

TIM. But I worked on the last one!

CHARLOTTE. Well so did I!

PIE SELLER. Don't look at me. I played two of 'em.

TIM. All right, all right, let's think about this. It's not a problem. We need a ghost, that's all. And he'll need some lines, and he has to be frightening, and he'll need a costume, and a little makeup, and he'll need some music and some really good lights *and he has to be ready in the next two minutes!*

CHARLOTTE. Don't panic!

TIM. I'M NOT PANICKING!

CHARLOTTE. *YOU ARE SO PANICKING!*

 (**TIM** *turns to the audience:*)

TIM. And then the strangest thing occurred…

 (*Ominous music plays and the lights change.*)

CHARLOTTE. Look!

BOOK SELLER. Look!

CHARLOTTE. Tim, who's that?!

TIM. I think it's the ghost.

CHARLOTTE. But I didn't… Honestly. I mean…

TIM. Neither did I.

 (*The clock tolls three and we hear the opening seconds of the First Movement of Mahler's Second Symphony in C Minor. The* **GHOST OF CHRISTMAS FUTURE** *appears. It is a puppet of dismal hue. The voice of the* **GHOST** *is augmented with a heavy reverb, making it echo deeply throughout the theatre.*)

GHOST OF CHRISTMAS FUTURE. Scroooooooge. Scroooooooge.

SCROOGE. *(frightened)* Who are you?

GHOST. I am the Ghost of Christmas Yet to Come.

SCROOGE. And where are you taking me?

GHOST. On the longest journey you will ever take. Come meet my friend.

Scene Seven.

(The Graveyard.)

GRAVEDIGGER. *(singing from The Messiah and digging)*
FOR BEHOLD,
DARKNESS SHALL COVER THE EARTH.
AND GROSS DARKNESS THE PEOPLE
AND GROSS DARKNESS THE PEOPLE...

SCROOGE. Who are you?

GRAVEDIGGER. Oh don't mind me. I'm not important. I'm just a gravedigger.

SCROOGE. A gravedigger? Is this a graveyard?

GRAVEDIGGER. Well let's see. Shovels. Dirt. Gravestones. Dead people. I'd say it's a graveyard. *Oh my back!* It's what you might call an occupational hazard.

SCROOGE. But why am I here?

GRAVEDIGGER. I have no idea. If you're here for a funeral, you're a little late. We just had one – and I've gotta tell ya, it was the strangest funeral I ever saw.

SCROOGE. Why is that?

GRAVEDIGGER. Because nobody came! Not a single person came to say good-bye to this here fella that I just buried. And he seemed perfectly normal to me when I saw him. Of course he was dead, but still. Two eyes, a nose, a mouth. Of course he wasn't usin' his nose and mouth cause he wasn't breathin'.

(He makes the face of a dead man.)

They said his name was Sneezer. Or Geezer.

SCROOGE. Ebenezer.

GRAVEDIGGER. That was it! Ebenezer Scrudge.

SCROOGE. Scrooge.

GRAVEDIGGER. Scrooge, that's right.

SCROOGE. And no one came to the funeral?

GRAVEDIGGER. Not a single soul. And yet to look at him, he could have been the nicest fella in the whole world. That mouth coulda smiled, right? Them eyes coulda twinkled now and then. So it must have been his attitude, do you know what I mean? It must have been what he felt in his heart. And that's really what it comes down to, don't it? What you feel in your heart for other people. If you help those less fortunate than you are, then you're a pretty good chap. But if you turn your back on 'em in their time of need, then you end up like this fella here, all shriveled and unhappy, and there's an end to it.

(**SCROOGE** *turns to the* **GHOST OF CHRISTMAS FUTURE***:*)

SCROOGE. O Spirit, tell me! Is it too late for me? Assure me that I yet may change these shadows by an altered life. I would live *so differently* with another chance. I would be kind and good and live a life for others. I would not turn my back on my fellow man, and I would do what I could for those in need. Tell me, Spirit: Can I be saved so that I may save others?

TIM. *(to the audience)* And all at once, a wind arose. A whole storm!

(*Crash! Music! The "Hallelujah Chorus" from The Messiah.*)

It was suddenly as if all Nature decided right then and there to give old Mr. Scrooge a second chance. And the wind picked him up and it flew him home,

SCROOGE. *Yaah! Yaaaaaah!*

TIM. and his door flew open and his pillow jumped right into place, and before you knew it, he was safe in his bed, all tucked up and back to sleep –

Scene Eight.

(Scrooge's bedroom.)

TIM. – until a boy appeared on the street below –

BOY. *(played by* **CHARLOTTE**, *ringing a bell)* "Merry Christmas! Merry Christmas!"

TIM. And it was Christmas morning, and suddenly one of Mr. Scrooge's eyes popped open… And then the other one…and he picked his head up off the pillow and he looked around…

SCROOGE. What do I feel? My fingers feel different. And my toes feel different. And my feet and my legs and my arms and my hands. I feel light as a feather and happy as an angel. I feel merry as a schoolboy and giddy as a colt!

BOY. And then he let out the biggest laugh you ever heard.

TIM. And for a man who had been out of practice for so many years, it was a splendid laugh,

BOY. an illustrious laugh,

TIM. the father of a long, long line of laughs.

SCROOGE. *Hahaaaaaaaaaaaaaaaaaaaaaaaa!*

(He walks around the edge of the stage shaking hands with everyone.)

Hello, how'dye do, nice to meet you, don't you look nice – hello, hello, hoo hoo, hello…

(Church bells ring.)

TIM. Then he ran to the window and threw it open and saw nothing but fresh clean air and a blanket of snow – and there on the street was a young man and his trusty sled.

SCROOGE. You! Young man. What is today, my fine little fellow?

BOY. Why it's Christmas morning, sir. We all know that.

SCROOGE. *(to himself)* I didn't miss it!

(to the **BOY***)*

Now listen to me: do you know the poultry seller at the corner?

BOY. Yes I do, sir.

SCROOGE. Do you know if they sold the prize turkey that was hanging in the window?

BOY. No they didn't, sir, for I just saw it.

SCROOGE. Excellent! Now go and buy it and have it delivered to the house of Bob and Martha Cratchit in Cripplegate. It'll cost two crowns, so I'm giving you four and you keep the rest.

BOY. Oh yes sir!

TIM. *(to the audience)* And then Scrooge dressed himself and shaved himself – though he almost cut his nose off with his razor he was so excited –

SCROOGE. *Ow!*

TIM. – and then he walked outdoors and made straight for the Cratchit house. But before he got there, he saw –

SCROOGE. Hollyfoot! Stevens! Listen to me – that charity you mentioned. I may have been a bit hasty, eh. So I'd like to give you…

(He whispers in their ears.)

HOLLYFOOT. How much?!

STEVENS. Lord bless me!

HOLLYFOOT. My dear Scrooge, are you being serious?

SCROOGE. Not a farthing less. A great many back payments are included in the sum, I assure you. But will you do me just one favor, sir.

STEVENS. Of course we will.

SCROOGE. Come and see me frequently. That's all I ask. Now I've got to hurry. I have a little trick to play on one of my friends. Merry Christmas!

TIM. *(to the audience)* And he left them standing dumbstruck in the snow and he made his way to the Cratchit house.

Scene Nine

(The Cratchit House. **SCROOGE** *knocks on the door severely. Bang, bang, bang!)*

BOB. C-coming. I'll be right there.

*(***BOB*** hurries to the door and opens it.)*

Mr. Scrooge! What are you...?

SCROOGE. *(acting angry) Cratchit?!*

BOB. Y-yes sir. Is something wrong, sir?

SCROOGE. *It's Christmas Day and you're not at the office!*

BOB. But sir, it's only seven o'clock. I'm-I'm-I'm still shaving and we don't open till nine o'clock and I can walk there in less than fifteen minutes –

MRS. CRATCHIT. Is that Mr. Scrooge?

EMILY. But it's only seven.

TIM. Good morning, sir.

SCROOGE. *That's not the point! It is not a good morning unless I say it is, and I'm not going to stand for this any longer! And therefore...*therefore...therefore, Bob –

(He can't help laughing.)

I'm raising your salary. No, I'm doubling it. And it will go up every year from this time on, and I have a turkey for you.

(The turkey appears and it's as big as a boy – it's huge! Meanwhile we hear the "Hallelujah Chorus" from The Messiah in the background.)

And presents and chestnuts and songs and good cheer, and listen to me very carefully: I will, from this moment on, endeavor to assist your family and give you all the things that you have justly earned.

TIM. Oh, Father!

CRATCHIT. Tim!

(They embrace.)

SCROOGE. And Tim will be well, I swear it on my life, and I only ask that you will forgive me for what I have done – and what I have been – for these many years, and I wish you Merry Christmas, Bob.

(He shakes their hands, one after another.)

And Mrs. Cratchit, and Emily, and Tim –

TIM. *(to the audience)* And Mr. Scrooge was as good as his word. He became our friend,

CHARLOTTE. and as good a man as any in the City.

PUPPET SELLER. And it was always said of him

PIE SELLER. that he knew how to keep the season well,

BOOK SELLER. and may that be truly said of all of us,

TIM. of *all* of us,

CHARLOTTE. be we Christian,

TIM. or Jewish,

PUPPET SELLER. or Muslim,

PIE SELLER. or Hindu,

BOOK SELLER. or black,

TIM. or white,

SCROOGE. or whatever you are and whatever you believe.

TIM. And so,

CHARLOTTE. as Tiny Tim observed one night,

TIM. when food was scarce,

CHARLOTTE. but spirits high:

TIM. God bless us every one.

(They all sing a reprise of "Deck the Halls" and wave good-bye.)

The End

www.ingramcontent.com/pod-product-compliance
Lightning Source LLC
Chambersburg PA
CBHW070421120726
47909CB00005B/1750